The Story of
Clan MacBleat

(The most doting Clan in Scotland)

Alison Mary Fitt & Keith Robson

Design - Melvin Creative
Printing - Printer Trento, Italy

Published by
GW Publishing
PO Box 6091
Thatcham
Berks
RG19 8XZ.

Tel + 44 (0)1635 268080
www.gwpublishing.com

ISBN 978-0-9561211-6-5

The Story of
Clan MacBleat

(The most doting clan in Scotland)

**If Scots words are new to you turn over and look,
you'll find them explained at the back of the book!**

Publishing

A long time ago, in the Highlands of Scotland, there lived a clan known as Clan MacBleat. They were called that because they absolutely doted on sheep.

In Glen Bleat, where they lived, they kept a very large flock, and the Clan Chief, Woolly Willie, and his clansmen, spoiled their sheep rotten. If they weren't patting them on their woolly heads, they were tickling their fleecy coats.

But this led to a problem. You see, Glen Bleat was mostly rough and stony, so there wasn't enough grass for the flock to graze on.

Sometimes, the sheep fought over every blade, while others did a runner.

Next morning, happy that the dyke was keeping their flock from straying, the MacBleats pulled up the last few turnips from their turnip field for the sheep's breakfast.

Suddenly ...

They were most upset to find that part of the dyke had collapsed.
Worse still, two sheep were leaping through the gap.
"It's Stephanie and Sasha," wailed Woolly Willie.

Back in their own glen, Clan MacBleat knitted woollen squares, from wool which they had spun from sheep's fleece, then dyed bright colours.

Woolly Willie's wife, Fleecy Fiona, who was an expert knitter, was in charge.

"In, out, over, off!" she chanted, as they all click-clacked away.

Woolly Willie hadn't knitted anything in his life, and neither had some of his clansmen, so their knitting soon got in a right old jumble.

Thankfully, Fleecy Fiona soon sorted their mistakes!

Once the squares were stitched together, Clan MacBleat had a braw, new, colourful picnic blanket to present to the MacScoffs.

The greedy clan were simply over the moon with it, and were so chuffed that they gladly forgave the MacBleats for what their sheep had done.
"That's a relief," sighed Willie. "From now on, we must stop any of our wee angels from straying!"

Unfortunately, parts of the shoogly dyke kept collapsing.
One day, the clansmen had just finished rebuilding a particular bit when they heard an almighty rumble.

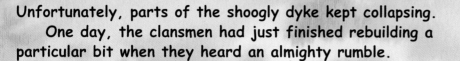

A section of dyke further down the sheep field, had given way and two more sheep dashed off.

After a long trot, the sheep found themselves in Glen Cauld, which was a horribly cold place indeed.

Clan MacShiver, who lived there, just couldn't get warm at all. Their teeth chattered and their noses were as red as rowan berries.

Even the grass was freezing cold, but the hungry sheep were still happy to chomp on it.

So, to put things right, Clan MacBleat held an all-night knitting session. And the next day, they were able to hand over lots of cosy, knitted woollies to the freezing MacShivers, who couldn't wait to put them on.

"We are all as warm as clootie dumplings now," chuckled Cauld Callum. "Let's say no more about your sheep's shenanigans!"

Woolly Willie was relieved to be forgiven once more.

"But we really must not let any more sheep escape," he warned his clansmen.

However, that was easier said than done because the dyke finally rumbled ... and tumbled ... then collapsed altogether.

With so many sheep, it was impossible to keep an eye on them all and soon another sheep wandered off into Glen Bonnie.

She quickly found herself in big trouble. For the "grass" she thought she was chewing on wasn't grass ... it was a wig which had been washed and left out to dry by Ronnie, the Chief of Clan Bonnie.

Luckily, the MacBleats were able to make up a wonderful new wig from some of their top-quality sheep fleece. Ronnie was thrilled to bits.

"It's a much grander wig than my other one," he beamed, as he preened in front of a mirror.

Woolly Willie tried to catch her but the sheep was too nifty on her hooves.

After leading him a merry dance, she charged over the drawbridge of a castle belonging to the ancient Earl of the Glens.

Nobody should drop in on an <u>Earl</u> without an invitation ... and certainly not a <u>sheep</u>!

Willie was horrified.

We're done for now!

As if that wasn't enough, the sheep plonked herself on the Earl's lap and started chewing his long, stringy hair. The Earl, who had been dozing, awoke with a start.

Willie felt sorry for the weary Earl.

"How about counting sheep?" he suggested, trying to be helpful.

The Earl was desperate to try anything, and agreed to give it a go.

"But I don't <u>keep</u> sheep, only deer!" he sighed.

"Not to worry," smiled Woolly Willie. "You can borrow some of ours."

However, the Earl went one better, and invited Clan MacBleat to flit their entire flock down to the castle grounds. Willie was delighted.

Back in Glen Bleat, the Chief gave his clansmen the good news.

The next day, the MacBleats led their flock to the castle grounds. The hungry sheep soon got down to some serious chewing and chomping, relieved not to be going back to the market.

Some words you need to know...

jist	just	neeps	turnips
kittled	tickled	tatties	potatoes
jinin	joining	oor	our
gie	give	whit	what
aboot	about	telt	told
yirsel	yourself	canna	can't
dinna	don't	hingin	hanging
guddled	messed up	oot	out
guid	good	drappin	dropping
wudna	wouldn't	ken	know
fechtin	fighting	heid buttin	head butting
awa	away	cauld	cold
shooglie	shaky	shouldna	shouldn't
hae	have	richt	right
		awfie	awful
		ye	you
		bubblin, greetin	crying
		well	weel
		lang	long
		sae	so
		auld	old

Woolly Willie explains...